T0019848

FUNERAL READINGS
AND POEMS

FUNERAL READINGS AND POEMS

Selection and preface by
BECKY BROWN

MACMILLAN COLLECTOR'S LIBRARY

This collection first published 2022 by Macmillan Collector's Library
an imprint of Pan Macmillan
The Smithson, 6 Briset Street, London EC1M 5NR
EU representative: Macmillan Publishers Ireland Ltd, 1st Floor,
The Liffey Trust Centre, 117–126 Sheriff Street Upper,
Dublin 1, D01 YC43
Associated companies throughout the world
www.panmacmillan.com

ISBN 978-1-5290-6540-4

Selection and preface © Becky Brown 2022

The permissions acknowledgements on pp.187–188 constitute
an extension of this copyright page.

3 5 7 9 8 6 4 2

A CIP catalogue record for this book is available from the British Library.

Cover and endpaper design: Mel Four, Pan Macmillan Art Department
Typeset in Plantin by Jouve (UK), Milton Keynes
Printed and bound in China by Imago

Visit **www.panmacmillan.com** to read more
about all our books and to buy them.

Contents

Preface xiii

FUNERAL BLUES

Funeral Blues *W. H. Auden* 3

from To Delia: On Her Endeavouring to Conceal
Her Grief at Parting *William Cowper* 5

'So, we'll go no more a-roving' *Lord Byron* 6

The Walk *Thomas Hardy* 7

Given in Farewell (To a girl of Yang-Chou)
Tu Mu tr. Don Paterson 8

from Letter to Miss Grace *Henry James* 9

Dirge without Music *Edna St. Vincent Millay* 10

from Letter to Miss Fanny Knight
Cassandra Austen 12

To The Beloved Dead: A Lament *Alice Meynell* 13

from De Profundis *Oscar Wilde* 15

Epitaph on monument erected in 1641
by Lady Catherine Dyer to her husband
Sir William Dyer in Colmworth Church,
Bedfordshire *Catherine Dyer* 16

Sea Canes *Derek Walcott* 17

To His Dying Brother, Master William Herrick
Robert Herrick 19

'A thousand years, you said'
Lady Heguri tr. Don Paterson 21

On Pain *Kahlil Gibran* 22

from King John *William Shakespeare* 23

from Anne of Green Gables
Lucy Maud Montgomery 24

'Silently I climb the Western Tower'
Li Yu tr. Don Paterson 26

from Letter to Calestrius Tiro
Pliny the Younger, tr. William Melmoth 27

from In Memoriam A. H. H. *Alfred,
Lord Tennyson* 29

To Stella *Percy Bysshe Shelley* 30

I Miss You *A. F. Harrold* 31

This, Too, Shall Pass Away *Lanta Wilson Smith* 33

from Agnes Grey *Anne Brontë* 35

LOVE LIVES BEYOND

Love Lives Beyond the Tomb *John Clare* 39

from Macbeth *William Shakespeare* 40

À quoi bon dire *Charlotte Mew* 41

from Letter to Rev. J. H. Twichell *Mark Twain* 42

No coward soul is mine *Emily Brontë* 43

Sonnet 71 *William Shakespeare* 45

from Letter from Norway *Mary Wollstonecraft* 46

from Walsinghame *Sir Walter Raleigh* 47

'They that love beyond the world' *William Penn* 48

from In Search of Lost Time *Marcel Proust* 49

'Bright is the ring of words' *Robert Louis Stevenson* 50

from Intimations of Immortality
William Wordsworth 51

from The Little Prince *Antoine de Saint-Exupéry* 52

Futility *Wilfred Owen* 54

'A slumber did my spirit steal'
William Wordsworth 55

Sorrow *D. H. Lawrence* 56

Music *Percy Bysshe Shelley* 57

from On Being Ill *Virginia Woolf* 58

To L. H. B. (1894–1915) *Katherine Mansfield* 59

Farewell my friends *Rabindranath Tagore* 60

Remember *Christina Rossetti* 62

Consolation *Elizabeth Barrett Browning* 63

A Pebble *James W. Foley* 64

Sonnet 30 *William Shakespeare* 67

After great pain a formal feeling comes
Emily Dickinson 68

Old Friendships *Samuel Johnson* 69

The Dead *Bernard Barton* 70

In Deep Thought, Gazing at the Moon *Li Po* 71

On Such a Day *Mary Coleridge* 72

A SUMMING UP

A Summing Up *Charles Mackay* 75

Nothing gold can stay *Robert Frost* 76

In Salutation to the Eternal Peace *Sarojini Naidu* 77

'Do not go gently into that good night'
Dylan Thomas 79

On Death *Kahlil Gibran* 81

Time is *Henry Van Dyke* 83

'Death is nothing at all' *Henry Scott Holland* 84

Epitaph on a Friend *Robert Burns* 85

Live Your Life
Chief Tecumseh of the Shawnee Nation 86

from Mrs Dalloway *Virginia Woolf* 88

Travelling *William Wordsworth* 89

from Letter to H. G. O. Blake, 3 April 1850
Henry David Thoreau 90

A Song *W. B. Yeats* 91

Happy the Man *John Dryden* 92

Solitude *Ella Wheeler Wilcox* 93

from Vanity Fair *William Makepeace Thackeray* 95

from A Shropshire Lad *A. E. Housman* 96

from The Water-Babies *Charles Kingsley* 100

Requiem *Robert Louis Stevenson* 101

'Not, how did he die, but how did he live?' *Anon.* 102

Prospice *Robert Browning* 103

Prayers *John Gould Fletcher* 104

IF DEATH IS KIND

If Death is Kind *Sara Teasdale* 111

from 'I loved her like the leaves'
Kakinomoto Hitomaro tr. Don Paterson 112

from The Tempest *William Shakespeare* 113

Continuities *Walt Whitman* 114

from 'The Song of Wandering Aengus' *W. B. Yeats* 115

from Life *Anna Laetitia Barbauld* 116

from War and Peace *Leo Tolstoy* 118

from Song of Myself *Walt Whitman* 119

from Little Women *Louisa May Alcott* 123

from In Memoriam, A. H. *Maurice Baring* 124

from Medley *Sarojini Naidu* 125

'Do not stand on my grave and weep' *Mary Frye* 126

'Bring us, o Lord God, at our last awakening'
John Donne 127

from Letter to Thomas Poole, April 6 1799
Samuel Taylor Coleridge 128

· ix ·

My Grave *Ella Wheeler Wilcox* 129

Birth and Death *Samuel Butler* 130

Lights out *Edward Thomas* 131

from One Day's List *Ford Madox Ford* 133

Heaven-Haven: A nun takes the veil
Gerard Manley Hopkins 134

There is a Field *Rumi* 135

from My Ántonia *Willa Cather* 136

from Adonais *Percy Bysshe Shelley* 137

from Cymbeline *William Shakespeare* 138

FREEDOM

Freedom *Olive Runner* 143

from Last Verses *Edmund Waller* 144

from In the Mountains *Elizabeth von Arnim* 145

Turn again *Mary Lee Hall* 146

In Blackwater Woods *Mary Oliver* 147

A Celtic blessing *Anon.* 149

Everything you see *Rumi* 150

Peace, my heart *Rabindranath Tagore* 151

Elegy Before Death *Edna St. Vincent Millay* 152

'Death stands above me' *Walter Savage Landor* 154

Farewell, sweet dust *Elinor Wylie* 155

No Funeral Gloom *Ellen Terry* 156

'Never weather-beaten Sail' *Thomas Campion* 157

Freedom *George William Russell* 158

'If I should go before the rest of you'
Joyce Grenfell 159

from The Wind in the Willows *Kenneth Grahame* 160

from The Old Curiosity Shop *Charles Dickens* 161

from Chamber Music *James Joyce* 162

from The Death of the Moth *Virginia Woolf* 163

from Peter Pan *J. M. Barrie* 166

Crossing the Bar *Alfred, Lord Tennyson* 167

Song *Christina Rossetti* 168

from In Memoriam A. H. H. *Alfred, Lord Tennyson* 169

'Why hold on to just one life' *Rumi* 170

To Every Thing There Is a Season
Book of Ecclesiastes 171

How Do I Love Thee?
Elizabeth Barrett Browning 172

from The Garden of Prosperine
Algernon Charles Swinburne 173

'I have seen death too often' *Anon.* 174

Index of Poets and Authors 175

Index of First Lines 179

Permissions acknowledgements 187

Preface
Becky Brown

Choosing a reading for a funeral or memorial service can feel incredibly daunting. A life, no matter how long or how short, is not an easy thing to sum up. Nor is the passing away of a loved one a universal experience that can be captured in one neatly all-embracing famous poem. The circumstances in which we lose people are many and various – whether it is a quiet slipping away in the extremity of old age, defeat after a hard-fought illness or a sudden bereavement – and each elicits an entirely different mode of grief.

The way we mourn as individuals is so complex and so personal that the chance of finding something truly *right*, a reading that captures every feeling, every angle and facet, can seem almost impossible. Yet the idea that someone else – whether a poet, writer or dramatist – might be better placed to speak accurately and perfectly to our personal pain, or offer a greater form of comfort than we can draw from our friends and families, can seem even more unlikely.

However, when we delve into the works of our great writers, there are many words of wisdom and solace to be found. Words as powerful, moving and thought-provoking today as when the ink first dried on the paper. The readings in this volume span centuries, continents, cultures, languages and religions. The writers – from William Shakespeare to Lucy Maud Montgomery, Rumi to Virginia Woolf – weave the ageless and universal thread of grief through the individual fabrics of their place and time. Their responses are as numerous as our own, channelling everything from bone-deep sorrow to white-hot anger, offering insight and consolation in equal measure. Each reading, whether written two thousand years ago or only a decade hence, has been chosen for the strength and truth of its feeling.

To help you find exactly the right words, the anthology is divided into five sections, each collecting together poems and prose with a similar tone and sentiment. Firstly, 'Funeral Blues', for readings that convey the overwhelming impact of grief, that mourn frankly and openly, without fear or moderation. Then, travelling from what is lost to what remains, 'Love Lives Beyond' for readings about the living impact of those no longer with us, and that speak to the importance and power of remembering. In 'A Summing Up' are words to celebrate a life well-lived, that rejoice in the pleasure of being on the earth, and that explore what it truly means to *live*. Moving on from happiness in life to peace beyond it, 'If Death is Kind' brings together readings that contemplate a better place – whether a heaven, an afterlife, a reincarnation or simply an end to suffering. And, finally, 'Freedom', for the distant end of grief, for the gentle relief of acceptance and letting go, for acknowledging the world in its new shape. Amongst them is an extract from A. C. Swinburne's poem *The Garden of Proserpine*:

> *We thank with brief thanksgiving*
> *Whatever gods may be*
> *That no life lives for ever;*
> *That dead men rise up never;*
> *That even the weariest river*
> *Winds somewhere safe to sea.*

There is something moving and meaningful in those lines. In the acceptance of life, death and everything between. Of the sense of a full circle with the beginning and the end flowing together, and finding peace.

FUNERAL BLUES

Funeral Blues

Stop all the clocks, cut off the telephone,
Prevent the dog from barking with a juicy
    bone,
Silence the pianos and with muffled drum
Bring out the coffin, let the mourners come.

Let aeroplanes circle moaning overhead
Scribbling on the sky the message He Is Dead,
Put crepe bows round the white necks of the
    public doves,
Let the traffic policemen wear black cotton
    gloves.

He was my North, my South, my East and
    West,
My working week and my Sunday rest,
My noon, my midnight, my talk, my song;
I thought that love would last for ever: I was
    wrong.

The stars are not wanted now: put out every
    one;
Pack up the moon and dismantle the sun;

Pour away the ocean and sweep up the wood;
For nothing now can ever come to any good.

W. H. Auden (1907–1973)

from To Delia: On Her Endeavouring to Conceal Her Grief at Parting

Hard is that heart, and unsubdued by love,
That feels no pain, nor ever heaves a sigh;
Such hearts the fiercest passions only prove,
Or freeze in cold insensibility.

Oh! then indulge thy grief, nor fear to tell
The gentle source from whence thy sorrows
  flow,
Nor think it weakness when we love to feel,
Nor think it weakness what we feel to show.

William Cowper (1731–1800)

'So, we'll go no more a-roving'

So, we'll go no more a-roving
So late into the night,
Though the heart be still as loving,
And the moon be still as bright.

For the sword outwears its sheath,
And the soul wears out the breast,
And the heart must pause to breathe,
And Love itself have rest.

Though the night was made for loving,
And the day returns too soon,
Yet we'll go no more a-roving
By the light of the moon.

Lord Byron (1788–1824)

The Walk

You did not walk with me
Of late to the hill-top tree
                    By the gated ways,
                    As in earlier days;
                    You were weak and lame,
          So you never came,
And I went alone, and I did not mind,
Not thinking of you as left behind.

          I walked up there to-day
          Just in the former way;
                    Surveyed around
                    The familiar ground
                    By myself again:
          What difference, then?
Only that underlying sense
Of the look of a room on returning thence.

Thomas Hardy (1840–1928)

Given in Farewell
(To a girl of Yang-Chou)

So deep in love, we seem without passion.
While we keep drinking, nothing shows.

Until the sky brightens
the candles will weep for us.

Tu Mu (China, 9th century),
translated by Don Paterson

from Letter to Miss Grace

We all live together, and those of us who love and know, live so most. We help each other – even unconsciously, each in our own effort, we lighten the effort of others, we contribute to the sum of success, make it possible for others to live. Sorrow comes in great waves – no one can know that better than you – but it rolls over us, and though it may almost smother us it leaves us on the spot, and we know that if it is strong we are stronger, inasmuch as it passes and we remain. It wears us, uses us, but we wear it and use it in return; and it is blind, whereas we after a manner see.

Henry James (1843–1916)

Dirge without Music

I am not resigned to the shutting away of
   loving hearts in the hard ground.
So it is, and so it will be, for so it has been,
   time out of mind:
Into the darkness they go, the wise and the
   lovely. Crowned
With lilies and with laurel they go; but I am
   not resigned.

Lovers and thinkers, into the earth with you.
Be one with the dull, the indiscriminate dust.
A fragment of what you felt, of what you knew,
A formula, a phrase remains, – but the best is
   lost.

The answers quick and keen, the honest look,
   the laughter, the love, –
They are gone. They are gone to feed the
   roses. Elegant and curled
Is the blossom. Fragrant is the blossom.
   I know. But I do not approve.
More precious was the light in your eyes than
   all the roses in the world.

Down, down, down into the darkness of the
  grave
Gently they go, the beautiful, the tender, the
  kind;
Gently they go, the intelligent, the witty, the
  brave
I know. But I do not approve. And I am not
  resigned.

Edna St. Vincent Millay (1892–1950)

from Letter to Miss Fanny Knight

I have lost a treasure, such a sister, such a friend as never can have been surpassed. She was the sun of my life, the gilder of every pleasure, the soother of every sorrow; I had not a thought concealed from her, and it is as if I had lost a part of myself.

Cassandra Austen (1773–1845)

To The Beloved Dead: A Lament

Beloved, thou art like a tune that idle fingers
    Play on a window-pane.
The time is there, the form of music lingers;
    But O thou sweetest strain,
Where is thy soul? Thou liest i' the wind and
    rain.

Even as to him who plays that idle air,
    It seems a melody,
For his own soul is full of it, so, my Fair,
    Dead, thou dost live in me,
And all this lonely soul is full of thee.

Thou song of songs!—not music as before
    Unto the outward ear;
My spirit sings thee inly evermore,
    Thy falls with tear on tear.
I fail for thee, thou art too sweet, too dear.

Thou silent song, thou ever voiceless rhyme,
    Is there no pulse to move thee
At windy dawn, with a wild heart beating
    time,

And falling tears above thee,
O music stifled from the ears that love thee?

Oh, for a strain of thee from outer air!
    Soul wearies soul, I find.
Of thee, thee, thee, I am mournfully aware,
    —Contained in one poor mind
Who wert in tune and time to every wind.

Poor grave, poor lost belovèd I but I burn
    For some more vast To be.
As he that played that secret tune may turn
    And strike it on a lyre triumphantly,
I wait some future, all a lyre for thee.

Alice Meynell (1847–1922)

from De Profundis

Prosperity, pleasure, and success, may be rough of grain and common in fibre, but sorrow is the most sensitive of all created things. There is nothing that stirs in the whole world of thought to which sorrow does not vibrate in terrible and exquisite pulsation. The thin beaten-out leaf of tremulous gold that chronicles the direction of forces the eye cannot see is in comparison coarse. It is a wound that bleeds when any hand but that of love touches it, and even then must bleed again, though not in pain.

Oscar Wilde (1854–1900)

Epitaph on monument erected
in 1641 by Lady Catherine Dyer
to her husband Sir William Dyer in
Colmworth Church, Bedfordshire

My dearest dust, could not thy hasty day
Afford thy drowzy patience leave to stay
One hower longer: so that we might either
sate up, or gone to bedd together?
But since thy finisht labor hath possest
Thy weary limbs with early rest,
Enjoy it sweetly: and thy widdowe bride
Shall soone repose her by thy slumbering side.
Whose business, now, is only to prepare
My nightly dress, and call to prayre:
Mine eyes wax heavy and ye day growes old.
The dew falls thick, my beloved growes cold.
Draw, draw ye closed curtaynes: and make
    room:
My dear, my dearest dust; I come, I come.

Catherine Dyer (c.1585–1654)

Sea Canes

Half my friends are dead.
I will make you new ones, said earth.
No, give me them back, as they were, instead,
with faults and all, I cried.

Tonight I can snatch their talk
from the faint surf's drone
through the canes, but I cannot walk

on the moonlit leaves of ocean
down that white road alone,
or float with the dreaming motion

of owls leaving earth's load.
O earth, the number of friends you keep
exceeds those left to be loved.

The sea canes by the cliff flash green and
   silver;
they were the seraph lances of my faith,
but out of what is lost grows something
   stronger

that has the rational radiance of stone,
enduring moonlight, further than despair,
strong as the wind, that through dividing
  canes

brings those we love before us, as they were,
with faults and all, not nobler, just there.

Derek Walcott (1930–2017)

To His Dying Brother,
Master William Herrick

Life of my life, take not so soone thy flight,
But stay the time till we have bade
   Good-night.
Thou hast both Wind and Tide with thee;
   Thy way
As soone dispatcht is by the Night, as Day.
Let us not then so rudely henceforth goe
Till we have wept, kist, sigh'd, shook hands,
   or so.
There's paine in parting; and a kind of hell,
When once true-lovers take their last
   Fare-well.
What? shall we two our endlesse leaves take
   here
Without a sad looke, or a solemne teare?
He knowes not Love, that hath not this truth
   proved,
Love is most loth to leave the thing beloved.
Pay we our Vowes, and goe; yet when we
   part,
Then, even then, I will bequeath my heart
Into thy loving hands: For Ile keep none

To warme my Breast, when thou my Pulse
    art gone.
No, here Ile last, and walk (a harmless shade)
About this Urne, wherein thy Dust is laid,
To guard it so, as nothing here shall be
Heavy, to hurt those sacred seeds of thee.

Robert Herrick (1591–1674)

'A thousand years, you said'

A thousand years, you said,
As our two hearts melted.
I look at the hand you held
And the ache is too hard to bear.

Lady Heguri (Japan, 8th century),
translated by Don Paterson

On Pain

from The Prophet

Your pain is the breaking of the shell that
   encloses your understanding.
Even as the stone of the fruit must break, that
   its heart may stand in the sun, so must you
   know pain.
And could you keep your heart in wonder at
   the daily miracles of your life, your pain
   would not seem less wondrous than your joy;
And you would accept the seasons of your
   heart, even as you have always accepted the
   seasons that pass over your fields.
And you would watch with serenity through
   the winters of your grief.

Kahlil Gibran (1883–1931)

from King John
Act III Scene IV

Grief fills the room up of my absent child:
Lies in his bed, walks up and down with me,
Puts on his pretty looks, repeats his words,
Remembers me of all his gracious parts,
Stuffs out his vacant garments with his form;
Then have I reason to be fond of grief!
Fare you well: had you such a loss as I,
I could give better comfort than you do.
I will not keep this form upon my head,
When there is such disorder in my wit . . .

William Shakespeare (1564–1616)

from Anne of Green Gables

Two days afterwards they carried Matthew Cuthbert over his homestead threshold and away from the fields he had tilled and the orchards he had loved and the trees he had planted; and then Avonlea settled back to its usual placidity and even at Green Gables affairs slipped into their old groove and work was done and duties fulfilled with regularity as before, although always with the aching sense of 'loss in all familiar things'. Anne, new to grief, thought it almost sad that it could be so – that they *could* go on in the old way without Matthew. She felt something like shame and remorse when she discovered that the sunrises behind the firs and the pale pink buds opening in the garden gave her the old inrush of gladness when she saw them – that Diana's visits were pleasant to her and that Diana's merry words and ways moved her to laughter and smiles – that, in brief, the beautiful world of blossom and love and friendship had lost none of its power to please her fancy and thrill her heart, that life still called to her with many insistent voices.

'It seems like disloyalty to Matthew, somehow, to find pleasure in these things now that he has gone,' she said wistfully to Mrs Allan one evening when they were together in the manse garden. 'I miss him so much – all the time – and yet, Mrs Allan, the world and life seem very beautiful and interesting to me for all. Today Diana said something funny and I found myself laughing. I thought when it happened I could never laugh again. And it somehow seems as if I oughtn't to.'

'When Matthew was here he liked to hear you laugh and he liked to know that you found pleasure in the pleasant things around you,' said Mrs Allan gently. 'He is just away now; and he likes to know it just the same. I am sure we should not shut our hearts against the healing influences that nature offers us. But I can understand your feeling. I think we all experience the same thing. We resent the thought that anything can please us when someone we love is no longer here to share the pleasure with us, and we almost feel as if we were unfaithful to our sorrow when we find our interest in life returning to us.'

Lucy Maud Montgomery (1874–1942)

'Silently I climb the Western Tower'

Silently I climb the Western Tower,
the moon a hook.
The Wu-t'ung trees in the deep courtyard
are closed by the cool Autumn.

That which scissors cannot sever,
And once unravelled is only knotted up again
Is the grief of parting
With a flavour for the heart all its own.

Li Yu (China, 10th century),
translated by Don Paterson

from Letter to Calestrius Tiro

I am every moment reflecting what a valuable friend, what an excellent man, I am deprived of. That he was arrived to his sixty-seventh year, which is an age even the strongest seldom exceed, I well know; that he is delivered from a life of continual pain; that he left his family and (what he loved even more) his country in a flourishing state: all this I know. Still I cannot forbear to lament him, as if he had been in the prime and vigour of his days; and I lament him (shall I own my weakness?) upon a private account. For I have lost, oh! my friend, I have lost the witness, the guide, and the governor of my life! And,—to confess to you as I did to Calvisius, in the first transport of my grief,—I sadly fear, now that I am no longer under his eye, I shall not keep so strict a guard over my conduct. Speak comfort to me, not that *he was old, he was infirm*: all this I know; but by supplying me with some reflections that are uncommon and resistless, that neither the commerce of the world, nor the precepts of the philosophers, can teach me. For all that I have heard, and all that I have read, occur to me of themselves; but all these are by far too weak to support me under so severe an affliction. Farewell.

Pliny the Younger (c.61–113),
translated by William Melmoth
the Younger (c.1710–1799)

from In Memoriam A. H. H.
LXXXVIII

Wild bird, whose warble, liquid sweet,
Rings Eden thro' the budded quicks,
O tell me where the senses mix,
O tell me where the passions meet,

Whence radiate: fierce extremes employ
Thy spirits in the darkening leaf,
And in the midmost heart of grief
Thy passion clasps a secret joy:

And I – my harp would prelude woe –
I cannot all command the strings;
The glory of the sum of things
Will flash along the chords and go.

Alfred, Lord Tennyson (1809–1892)

To Stella

Thou wert the morning star among the living,
    Ere thy fair light had fled;—
Now, having died, thou art as Hesperus,
  giving
    New splendour to the dead.

Percy Bysshe Shelley (1792–1822)

I Miss You

I miss you
Like the puddle misses the snowman it was

I miss you like the butterfly misses the
   caterpillar
Like the frog misses the tadpole
Like the penguin misses the warm egg

I miss you
Like my desk misses the tree it was before it
   was my desk

I miss you
Like the oak tree misses the acorn it grew
   from
Like the silence misses the song
Like the book misses the blank page

I miss you
Like the surprise misses still being a surprise

Like the sailor misses the land
Like the astronaut misses the earth

Like the grown-up misses being the child
Like the arrow misses the bow it's shot from

I miss you like I miss you.

A. F. Harrold (1975–)

This, Too, Shall Pass Away

When some great sorrow like a mighty river,
Flows through your life with peace-destroying
   power,
And dearest things are swept from sight
   forever,
Say to your heart each trying hour:
'This, too, shall pass away.'

When ceaseless toil has hushed your song of
   gladness,
And you have grown almost too tired to pray,
Let this truth banish from your heart its
   sadness,
And ease the burdens of each trying day:
'This, too, shall pass away.'

When fortune smiles, and, full of mirth and
   pleasure,
The days are flitting by without a care,
Lest you should rest with only earthly
   treasure,
Let these few words their fullest import bear:
'This, too, shall pass away.'

When earnest labor brings you fame and glory,
And all earth's noblest ones upon you smile,
Remember that life's longest, grandest story
Fills but a moment in earth's little while:
'This, too, shall pass away.'

Lanta Wilson Smith (1856–1939)

from Agnes Grey

'O, they have robbed me of the hope
My spirit held so dear;
They will not let me hear that voice
My soul delights to hear.

'They will not let me see that face
I so delight to see;
And they have taken all thy smiles,
And all thy love from me.

'Well, let them seize on all they can; –
One treasure still is mine, –
A heart that loves to think on thee,
And feels the worth of thine.'

Anne Brontë (1820–1849)

LOVE LIVES BEYOND

Love Lives Beyond the Tomb

Love lives beyond the tomb
And earth, which fades like dew!
I love the fond,
The faithful, and the true.

Love lives in sleep:
'Tis happiness of healthy dreams;
Eve's dews may weep,
But love delightful seems.

'Tis seen in flowers,
And in the morning's pearly dew;
In earth's green hours,
And in the heaven's eternal blue.

'Tis heard in Spring
When light and sunbeams, warm and kind,
On angel's wing
Bring love and music to the mind . . .

John Clare (1793–1864)

from Macbeth

To-morrow, and to-morrow, and to-morrow,
Creeps in this petty pace from day to day.
To the last syllable of recorded time;
And all our yesterdays have lighted fools
The way to dusty death. Out, out, brief
   candle!
Life's but a walking shadow; a poor player,
That struts and frets his hour upon the stage,
And then is heard no more: it is a tale
Told by an idiot, full of sound and fury,
Signifying nothing.

William Shakespeare (1564–1616)

À quoi bon dire

Seventeen years ago you said
    Something that sounded like Good-bye;
    And everybody thinks you are dead,
        But I.

    So I, as I grow stiff and cold
To this and that say Good-bye too;
    And everybody sees that I am old
        But you.

    And one fine morning in a sunny lane
Some boy and girl will meet and kiss and
  swear
    That nobody can love their way again
        While over there
You will have smiled, I shall have tossed your
  hair.

Charlotte Mew (1869–1928)

from Letter to Rev. J. H. Twichell

This is our day of mourning. It is four years since Susy died; it is five years and a month that I saw her alive for the last time—throwing kisses at us from the railway platform when we started West around the world. Sometimes it is a century; sometimes it was yesterday.

Mark Twain (1835–1910)

No coward soul is mine

No coward soul is mine
No trembler in the world's storm-troubled
  sphere
I see Heaven's glories shine
And Faith shines equal arming me from Fear

O God within my breast
Almighty ever-present Deity
Life, that in me hast rest
As I Undying Life, have power in thee

Vain are the thousand creeds
That move men's hearts, unutterably vain,
Worthless as withered weeds
Or idlest froth amid the boundless main

To waken doubt in one
Holding so fast by thy infinity
So surely anchored on
The steadfast rock of Immortality

With wide-embracing love
Thy spirit animates eternal years

Pervades and broods above,
Changes, sustains, dissolves, creates and rears

Though Earth and moon were gone
And suns and universes ceased to be
And thou wert left alone
Every Existence would exist in the

There is not room for Death
Nor atom that his might cou   render void
Since thou art Being and Br   h
And what thou art may nev   e destroyed

Em   ronté (1818–1848)

Sonnet 71

No longer mourn for me when I am dead
Than you shall hear the surly sullen bell
Give warning to the world that I am fled
From this vile world, with vilest worms to
   dwell:
Nay, if you read this line, remember not
The hand that writ it; for I love you so,
That I in your sweet thoughts would be forgot,
If thinking on me then should make you woe.
O, if, I say, you look upon this verse
When I perhaps compounded am with clay,
Do not so much as my poor name rehearse;
But let your love even with my life decay;
     Lest the wise world should look into your
      moan,
     And mock you with me after I am gone.

William Shakespeare (1564–1616)

from Letter from Norway

The pine and fir woods, left entirely to Nature, display an endless variety; and the paths in the woods are not entangled with fallen leaves, which are only interesting whilst they are fluttering between life and death. The grey cobweb-like appearance of the aged pines is a much finer image of decay; the fibres whitening as they lose their moisture, imprisoned life seems to be stealing away. I cannot tell why, but death, under every form, appears to me like something getting free—to expand in I know not what element—nay, I feel that this conscious being must be as unfettered, have the wings of thought, before it can be happy.

Mary Wollstonecraft (1759–1797)

from Walsinghame

. . . But true love is a durable fire,
    In the mind ever burning,
Never sick, never dead, never cold,
    From itself never turning.

Sir Walter Raleigh (1552–1618)

'They that love beyond the world'

They that love beyond the world, cannot be
  separated by it.
Death cannot kill what never dies.
Nor can spirits ever be divided that love and
  live in the same divine
    principle, the root and record of their
    friendship.
If absence be not death, neither is theirs.
Death is but crossing the world, as friends do
  the seas; they live in one another still.
For they must needs be present, that love and
  live in that which is omnipresent.
This is the comfort of friends, that though
  they may be said to die,
    yet their friendship and society are ever
    present, because immortal.

William Penn (1644–1718)

from In Search of Lost Time

We say at times that something may survive of a man after his death, if the man was an artist and took a certain amount of pains with his work. It is perhaps in the same way that a sort of cutting taken from one person and grafted on the heart of another continues to carry on its existence, even when the person from whom it had been detached has perished.

Marcel Proust (1871–1922)

'Bright is the ring of words'

Bright is the ring of words
When the right man rings them,
Fair the fall of songs
When the singer sings them.
Still they are carolled and said –
On wings they are carried –
After the singer is dead
And the maker buried.

Robert Louis Stevenson (1850–1894)

from Intimations of Immortality

What though the radiance which was once
  so bright
Be now for ever taken from my sight,
    Though nothing can bring back the hour
Of splendour in the grass, of glory in the
  flower;
      We will grieve not, rather find
      Strength in what remains behind;

William Wordsworth (1770–1850)

from The Little Prince

'People have stars but they're not all the same.
For those who travel, the stars are guides. For
others, they are nothing but little lights. For
others, who are scientists, they are prob-
lems. For my businessman they were gold.
Those stars are all silent. But you will have stars
that are completely different . . .'

'What do you mean?'

'When you look at the sky at night, because
I'll be living on one of them, because I'll be
laughing on one of them, to you it will sound as
if all the stars are laughing. You will have stars
that can laugh!'

And he laughed again.

'And when you have found consolation – as
people always do – you will be glad to have
known me. You will always be my friend.
You'll want to laugh with me. And sometimes
you will open your window, just like that, for
the pleasure . . . and your friends will be aston-
ished to see you looking at the sky and laughing.
They you'll say to them: "Yes, the stars always
make me laugh!" and they'll think you're

mad. What a mischievous trick I'll have played
on you.'

Antoine de Saint-Exupéry (1900–1944)

Futility

Move him into the sun –
Gently its touch awoke him once,
At home, whispering of fields half-sown.
Always it woke him, even in France,
Until this morning and this snow.
If anything might rouse him now
The kind old sun will know.

Think how it wakes the seeds
Woke once the clays of a cold star.
Are limbs, so dear-achieved, are sides
Full-nerved, still warm, too hard to stir?
Was it for this the clay grew tall?
– O what made fatuous sunbeams toil
To break earth's sleep at all?

Wilfred Owen (1893–1918)

'A slumber did my spirit seal'

A slumber did my spirit seal;
I had no human fears:
She seemed a thing that could not feel
The touch of earthly years.

No motion has she now, no force;
She neither hears nor sees;
Rolled round in earth's diurnal course,
With rocks, and stones, and trees.

William Wordsworth (1770–1850)

Sorrow

Why does the thin grey strand
Floating up from the forgotten
Cigarette between my fingers,
Why does it trouble me?

Ah, you will understand;
When I carried my mother downstairs,
A few times only, at the beginning
Of her soft-foot malady,

I should find, for a reprimand
To my gaiety, a few long grey hairs
On the breast of my coat; and one by one
I let them float up the dark chimney.

D. H. Lawrence (1885–1930)

Music

Music, when soft voices die,
Vibrates in the memory –
Odours, when sweet violets sicken,
Live within the sense they quicken.
Rose leaves, when the rose is dead,
Are heaped for the beloved's bed;
And so thy thoughts, when thou art gone,
Love itself shall slumber on.

Percy Bysshe Shelley (1792–1822)

from On Being Ill

It is only the recumbent who know what, after all, nature is at no pains to conceal—that she in the end will conquer; the heat will leave the world; stiff with frost we shall cease to drag our feet about the fields; ice will lie thick upon factory and engine; the sun will go out. Even so, when the whole earth is sheeted and slippery some undulation, some irregularity of surface will mark the boundary of an ancient garden, and there, thrusting its head up undaunted in the starlight, the rose will flower, the crocus will burn.

Virginia Woolf (1882–1941)

To L. H. B. (1894–1915)

Last night for the first time since you were
  dead
I walked with you, my brother, in a dream.
We were at home again beside the stream
Fringed with tall berry bushes, white and red.
'Don't touch them: they are poisonous,' I said.
But your hand hovered, and I saw a beam
Of strange, bright laughter flying round your
  head
And as you stooped I saw the berries gleam.
'Don't you remember? We called them Dead
  Man's Bread!'
I woke and heard the wind moan and the roar
Of the dark water tumbling on the shore.
Where – where is the path of my dream for my
  eager feet?
By the remembered stream my brother stands
Waiting for me with berries in his hands . . .
'These are my body. Sister, take and eat.'

Katherine Mansfield (1888–1923)

Farewell my friends

It was beautiful
As long as it lasted
The journey of my life.

I have no regrets
Whatsoever save
The pain I'll leave behind.
Those dear hearts
Who love and care . . .
And the strings pulling
At the heart and soul . . .

The strong arms
That held me up
When my own strength
Let me down.

At every turning of my life
I came across
Good friends,
Friends who stood by me
Even when the time raced me by.

Farewell, farewell
My friends
I smile and
Bid you goodbye.
No, shed no tears
For I need them not
All I need is your smile.

If you feel sad
Do think of me
For that's what I'll like
When you live in the hearts
Of those you love
Remember then
You never die.

Rabindranath
Tagore (1861–1941)

Remember

Remember me when I am gone away,
Gone far away into the silent land;
When you can no more hold me by the hand,
Nor I half turn to go, yet turning stay.
Remember me when no more day by day
You tell me of our future that you planned:
Only remember me; you understand
It will be late to counsel then or pray.
Yet if you should forget me for a while
And afterwards remember, do not grieve:
For if the darkness and corruption leave
A vestige of the thoughts that once I had,
Better by far you should forget and smile
Than that you should remember and be sad.

Christina Rossetti (1830–1894)

Consolation

All are not taken; there are left behind
Living Beloveds, tender looks to bring
And make the daylight still a happy thing,
And tender voices, to make soft the wind:
But if it were not so – if I could find
No love in all this world for comforting,
Nor any path but hollowly did ring
Where 'dust to dust' the love from life
  disjoin'd;
And if, before those sepulchres unmoving
I stood alone (as some forsaken lamb
Goes bleating up the moors in weary dearth)
Crying 'Where are ye, O my loved and loving?' –
I know a voice would sound, 'Daughter, I am.
Can I suffice for Heaven and not for earth?'

Elizabeth Barrett Browning (1806–1861)

A Pebble

Drop a pebble in the water: just a splash, and
   it is gone;
But there's half-a-hundred ripples circling on
   and on and on,
Spreading, spreading from the center, flowing
   on out to the sea.
And there is no way of telling where the end is
   going to be.

Drop a pebble in the water: in a minute you
   forget,
But there's little waves a-flowing, and there's
   ripples circling yet,
And those little waves a-flowing to a great big
   wave have grown;
You've disturbed a mighty river just by
   dropping in a stone.

Drop an unkind word, or careless: in a minute
   it is gone;
But there's half-a-hundred ripples circling on
   and on and on.

They keep spreading, spreading, spreading
   from the center as they go,
And there is no way to stop them, once you've
   started them to flow.

Drop an unkind word, or careless: in a minute
   you forget;
But there's little waves a-flowing, and there's
   ripples circling yet,
And perhaps in some sad heart a mighty wave
   of tears you've stirred,
And disturbed a life was happy ere you
   dropped that unkind word.

Drop a word of cheer and kindness: just a
   flash and it is gone;
But there's half-a-hundred ripples circling on
   and on and on,
Bearing hope and joy and comfort on each
   splashing, dashing wave
Till you wouldn't believe the volume of the
   one kind word you gave.

Drop a word of cheer and kindness: in a
   minute you forget;

But there's gladness still a-swelling, and
  there's joy circling yet,
And you've rolled a wave of comfort whose
  sweet music can be heard
Over miles and miles of water just by dropping
  one kind word.

James W. Foley (1874–1939)

Sonnet 30

When to the sessions of sweet silent thought
I summon up remembrance of things past,
I sigh the lack of many a thing I sought,
And with old woes new wail my dear times'
    waste:
Then can I drown an eye, unus'd to flow,
For precious friends hid in death's dateless
    night,
And weep afresh love's long-since-cancell'd
    woe,
And moan the expense of many a vanish'd
    sight:
Then can I grieve at grievances foregone,
And heavily from woe to woe tell o'er
The sad account of fore-bemoaned moan,
Which I new pay as if not paid before.
    But if the while I think on thee, dear friend,
    All losses are restor'd, and sorrows end.

William Shakespeare (1564–1616)

After great pain a formal feeling comes

After great pain a formal feeling comes –
The nerves sit ceremonious like tombs;
The stiff Heart questions – was it He that bore?
And yesterday – or centuries before?

The feet mechanical
Go round a wooden way
Of ground or air or Ought, regardless grown,
A quartz contentment like a stone.

This is the hour of lead
Remembered if outlived,
As freezing persons recollect the snow –
First chill, then stupor, then the letting go.

Emily Dickinson (1830–1886)

Old Friendships

Those that have loved longest love best. A sudden blaze of kindness may, by a single blast of coldness, be extinguished; but that fondness which length of time has connected with many circumstances and occasions, though it may for a while be suppressed by disgust or resentment, with or without a cause, is hourly revived by accidental recollection. To those that have lived long together, every thing heard and every thing seen, recals some pleasure communicated, or some benefit conferred, some petty quarrel, or some slight endearment. Esteem of great powers, or amiable qualities newly discovered, may embroider a day or a week; but a friendship of twenty years is interwoven with the texture of life. A friend may be often found and lost; but an *old friend* never can be found, and nature has provided that he cannot easily be lost.

Samuel Johnson (1709–1784)

The Dead

The dead are like the stars by day,
    Withdrawn from mortal eye,
Yet holding unperceived their way
    Through the unclouded sky.

By them, through holy hope and love,
    We feel in hours serene,
Connected with a world above,
    Immortal and unseen.

For Death his sacred seal hath set
    On bright and bygone hours;
And they we mourn are with us yet,
    Are more than ever ours;—

Ours by the pledge of love and faith,
    By hopes of heaven on high;
By trust triumphant over death,
    In immortality.

Bernard Barton (1784–1849)

In Deep Thought, Gazing at the Moon

The clear spring reflects the thin, wide-
     spreading pine-tree—
And for how many thousand, thousand years?
No one knows.
The late Autumn moon shivers along the little
     water ripples,
The brilliance of it flows in through the
     window.
Before it I sit for a long time absent-mindedly
     chanting,
Thinking of my friend—
What deep thoughts!
There is no way to see him. How then can we
     speak together?
Joy is dead. Sorrow is the heart of man.

Li Po (c.700–762)

On Such a Day

Some hang above the tombs,
Some weep in empty rooms,
I, when the iris blooms,
    Remember.

I, when the cyclamen
Opens her buds again,
Rejoice a moment – then
    Remember.

Mary Coleridge (1861–1907)

A SUMMING UP

A Summing Up

I have lived and I have loved;
I have waked and I have slept;
I have sung and I have danced;
I have smiled and I have wept;
I have won and wasted treasure;
I have had my fill of pleasure;
And all these things were weariness,
And some of them were dreariness,
And all these things, but two things,
Were emptiness and pain:
And Love – it was the best of them;
And Sleep – worth all the rest of them.

Charles Mackay (1814–1889)

Nothing gold can stay

Nature's first green is gold,
Her hardest hue to hold.
Her early leaf's a flower;
But only so an hour.
Then leaf subsides to leaf.
So Eden sank to grief,
So dawn goes down to day.
Nothing gold can stay.

Robert Frost (1874–1963)

In Salutation to the Eternal Peace

Men say the world is full of fear and hate,
And all life's ripening harvest-fields await
The restless sickle of relentless fate.

But I, sweet Soul, rejoice that I was born,
When from the climbing terraces of corn
I watch the golden orioles of Thy morn.

What care I for the world's desire and pride,
Who know the silver wings that gleam and
    glide,
The homing pigeons of Thine eventide?

What care I for the world's loud weariness,
Who dream in twilight granaries Thou dost
    bless
With delicate sheaves of mellow silences?

Say, shall I heed dull presages of doom,
Or dread the rumoured loneliness and
    gloom,
The mute and mythic terror of the tomb?

For my glad heart is drunk and drenched with
  Thee,
O inmost wine of living ecstasy !
O intimate essence of eternity !

Sarojini Naidu (1879–1949)

'Do not go gentle into that good night'

Do not go gentle into that good night,
Old age should burn and rave at close of day;
Rage, rage against the dying of the light.

Though wise men at their end know dark is
   right,
Because their words had forked no lightning
   they
Do not go gentle into that good night.

Good men, the last wave by, crying how bright
Their frail deeds might have danced in a green
   bay,
Rage, rage against the dying of the light.

Wild men who caught and sang the sun in flight,
And learn, too late, they grieved it on its way,
Do not go gentle into that good night.

Grave men, near death, who see with blinding
   sight
Blind eyes could blaze like meteors and be gay,
Rage, rage against the dying of the light.

And you, my father, there on the sad height,
Curse, bless, me now with your fierce tears,
   I pray.
Do not go gentle into that good night.
Rage, rage against the dying of the light.

Dylan Thomas (1914–1953)

On Death

from The Prophet

You would know the secret of death.

But how shall you find it unless you seek it in
  the heart of life?

The owl whose night-bound eyes are blind
  unto the day cannot unveil the mystery of
  light.

If you would indeed behold the spirit of death,
  open your heart wide unto the body of life.

For life and death are one, even as the river
  and the sea are one.

In the depth of your hopes and desires lies
  your silent knowledge of the beyond;

And like seeds dreaming beneath the snow
  your heart dreams of spring.

Trust the dreams, for in them is hidden the
  gate to eternity.

Your fear of death is but the trembling of the
  shepherd when he stands before the king
  whose hand is to be laid
      upon him in honour.

Is the shepherd not joyful beneath his trembling,
   that he shall wear the mark of the king?
Yet is he not more mindful of his trembling?

For what is it to die but to stand naked in the
   wind and to melt into the sun?
And what is it to cease breathing but to free
   the breath from its restless tides, that it may
   rise and expand and seek
      God unencumbered?

Only when you drink from the river of silence
   shall you indeed sing.
And when you have reached the mountain top,
   then you shall begin to climb.
And when the earth shall claim your limbs,
   then shall you truly dance.

Kahlil Gibran (1883–1931)

Time is

Time is too slow for those who wait,
too swift for those who fear,
too long for those who grieve,
too short for those who rejoice;
but for those who love, time is eternity.

Henry Van Dyke (1852–1933)

'Death is nothing at all'

Death is nothing at all. I have only slipped away into the next room. I am I, and you are you. Whatever we were to each other, that we still are. Call me by my old familiar name, speak to me in the easy way that you always used. Put no difference in your tone, wear no forced air of solemnity or sorrow. Laugh as we always laughed at the little jokes we enjoyed together. Play, smile, think of me, pray for me. Let my name be ever the household word that it always was, let it be spoken without effect, without the trace of a shadow on it.

Life means all that it ever meant. It is the same as it ever was; there is unbroken continuity. Why should I be out of mind because I am out of sight? I am waiting for you, for an interval, somewhere very near, just round the corner.

All is well.

Henry Scott Holland (1847–1918)

Epitaph on a Friend

An honest man here lies at rest,
The friend of man, the friend of truth,
The friend of age, and guide of youth:
Few hearts like his, with virtue warm'd,
Few heads with knowledge so inform'd;
If there's another world, he lives in bliss;
If there is none, he made the best of this.

Robert Burns (1759–1796)

Live Your Life

Live your life that the fear of death
can never enter your heart.
Trouble no one about his religion.
Respect others in their views
and demand that they respect yours.
Love your life, perfect your life,
beautify all things in your life.
Seek to make your life long
and of service to your people.
Prepare a noble death song for the day
when you go over the great divide.
Always give a word or sign of salute when
   meeting
or passing a friend, or even a stranger, if in a
   lonely place.
Show respect to all people but grovel to none.
When you rise in the morning, give thanks for
   the light,
for your life, for your strength.
Give thanks for your food and for the joy of
   living.
If you see no reason to give thanks,
the fault lies in yourself.

Touch not the poisonous firewater that makes
   wise ones turn to fools
and robs the spirit of its vision.
When your time comes to die, be not like
   those
whose hearts are filled with fear of death,
so that when their time comes they weep and
   pray
for a little more time to live their lives over
   again
in a different way.
Sing your death song, and die like a hero
   going home.

Chief Tecumseh of the
Shawnee Nation (1768–1813)

from Mrs Dalloway

Did it matter then, she asked herself, walking towards Bond Street, did it matter that she must inevitably cease completely; all this must go on without her; did she resent it; or did it not become consoling to believe that death ended absolutely? but that somehow in the streets of London, on the ebb and flow of things, here, there, she survived, Peter survived, lived in each other, she being part, she was positive, of the trees at home; of the house there, ugly, rambling all to bits and pieces as it was; part of people she had never met; being laid out like a mist between the people she knew best, who lifted her on their branches as she had seen the trees lift the mist, but it spread ever so far, her life, herself.

Virginia Woolf (1882–1941)

Travelling

This is the spot: – how mildly does the sun
Shine in between the fading leaves! the air
In the habitual silence of this wood
Is more than silent: and this bed of heath,
Where shall we find so sweet a resting-place?
Come! – let me see thee sink into a dream
Of quiet thoughts, – protracted till thine eye
Be calm as water when the winds are gone
And no one can tell whither – my sweet friend!
We two have had such happy hours together
That my heart melts in me to think of it.

William Wordsworth (1770–1850)

from Letter to H. G. O. Blake,
3 April 1850

I am not afraid that I shall exaggerate the value
and significance of life, but that I shall not be
up to the occasion which it is. I shall be sorry to
remember that I was there, but noticed nothing
remarkable,—not so much as a prince in dis-
guise; lived in the golden age a hired man;
visited Olympus even, but fell asleep after
dinner, and did not hear the conversation of the
gods.

Henry David Thoreau (1817–1862)

A Song

I thought no more was needed
Youth to prolong
Than dumb-bell and foil
To keep the body young.
O who could have foretold
That the heart grows old?

Though I have many words,
What woman's satisfied,
I am no longer faint
Because at her side?
O who could have foretold
That the heart grows old?

I have not lost desire
But the heart that I had;
I thought 'twould burn my body
Laid on the death-bed,
For who could have foretold
That the heart grows old?

W. B. Yeats (1865–1939)

Happy the Man

Happy the man, and happy he alone,
    He who can call today his own;
He who, secure within, can say,
    Tomorrow, do thy worst, for I have lived
    today.

John Dryden (1631–1700)

Solitude

Laugh, and the world laughs with you;
  Weep, and you weep alone,
For sad old earth must borrow its mirth,
  But has trouble enough of its own.
Sing, and the hills will answer;
  Sigh, it is lost on the air,
The echoes bound to a joyful sound,
  But shrink from voicing care.

Rejoice, and men will seek you;
  Grieve, and they turn and go.
They want full measure of all your pleasure.
  But they do not need your woe.
Be glad, and your friends are many;
  Be sad, and you lose them all—
There are none to decline your nectar'd wine,
  But alone you must drink life's gall.

Feast, and your halls are crowded;
  Fast, and the world goes by.
Succeed and give, and it helps you live,
  But no man can help you die.
There is room in the halls of pleasure

For a large and lordly train,
But one by one we must all file on
Through the narrow aisles of pain.

Ella Wheeler Wilcox (1850–1919)

from Vanity Fair

The world is a looking-glass, and gives back to every man the reflection of his own face. Frown at it, and it will in turn look sourly upon you; laugh at it and with it, and it is a jolly, kind companion . . .

William Makepeace Thackeray (1811–1863)

from A Shropshire Lad

The Merry Guide

Once in the wind of morning
    I ranged the thymy wold;
The world-wide air was azure
    And all the brooks ran gold.

There through the dews beside me
    Behold a youth that trod,
With feathered cap on forehead,
    And poised a golden rod.

With mien to match the morning
    And gay delightful guise
And friendly brows and laughter
    He looked me in the eyes.

Oh whence, I asked, and whither?
    He smiled and would not say,
And looked at me and beckoned
    And laughed and led the way.

And with kind looks and laughter
    And nought to say beside
We two went on together,
    I and my happy guide.

Across the glittering pastures
    And empty upland still
And solitude of shepherds
    High in the folded hill,

By hanging woods and hamlets
    That gaze through orchards down
On many a windmill turning
    And far-discovered town,

With gay regards of promise
    And sure unslackened stride
And smiles and nothing spoken
    Led on my merry guide.

By blowing realms of woodland
    With sunstruck vanes afield
And cloud-led shadows sailing
    About the windy weald,

By valley-guarded granges
    And silver waters wide,
Content at heart I followed
    With my delightful guide.

And like the cloudy shadows
    Across the country blown
We two fare on for ever,
    But not we two alone.

With the great gale we journey
    That breathes from gardens thinned,
Borne in the drift of blossoms
    Whose petals throng the wind;

Buoyed on the heaven-heard whisper
    Of dancing leaflets whirled
From all the woods that autumn
    Bereaves in all the world.

And midst the fluttering legion
    Of all that ever died
I follow, and before us
    Goes the delightful guide,

With lips that brim with laughter
   But never once respond,
      And feet that fly on feathers,
         And serpent-circled wand.

A. E. Housman (1859–1936)

from The Water-Babies

When all the world is young, lad,
　　And all the trees are green;
And every goose a swan, lad,
　　And every lass a queen;
Then hey for boot and horse, lad,
　　And round the world away;
Young blood must have its course, lad,
　　And every dog his day.

When all the world is old, lad,
　　And all the trees are brown;
And all the sport is stale, lad,
　　And all the wheels run down;
Creep home, and take your place there,
　　The spent and maimed among:
God grant you find one face there,
　　You loved when all was young.

Charles Kingsley (1819–1875)

Requiem

Under the wide and starry sky,
Dig the grave and let me lie.
Glad did I live and gladly die,
And I laid me down with a will.

This be the verse you grave for me:
Here he lies where he longed to be;
Home is the sailor, home from sea,
And the hunter home from the hill.

Robert Louis Stevenson (1850–1894)

'Not, how did he die, but how did he live?'

Not, how did he die, but how did he live?
Not, what did he gain, but what did he give?
These are the units to measure the worth
Of a man as a man, regardless of birth.
Not what was his church, nor what was his
　creed?
But had he befriended those really in need?
Was he ever ready, with word of good cheer,
To bring back a smile, to banish a tear?
Not what did the sketch in the newspaper say,
But how many were sorry when he passed
　away?

Anon.

Prospice

Fear death?—to feel the fog in my throat,
    The mist in my face,
When the snows begin, and the blasts denote
    I am nearing the place,
The power of the night, the press of the storm,
    The post of the foe;
Where he stands the Arch Fear in a visible form,
    Yet the strong man must go:
For the journey is done and the summit attained,
    And the barriers fall,
Though a battle's to fight ere the guerdon be
gained,
    The reward of it all.
I was ever a fighter, so—one fight more,
    The best and the last!
I would hate that death bandaged my eyes,
and forebore,
    And bade me creep past.
No! let me taste the whole of it, fare like my
peers
    The heroes of old,
Bear the brunt, in a minute pay glad life's
arrears

Of pain, darkness and cold.
For sudden the worst turns the best to the
    brave,
        The black minute's at end,
And the elements' rage, the fiend-voices that
    rave,
        Shall dwindle, shall blend,
Shall change, shall become first a peace out of
    pain,
        Then a light, then thy breast,
O thou soul of my soul! I shall clasp thee
    again,
        And with God be the rest!

Robert Browning (1812–1889)

Prayers

I

Let the wind come,
And cover our feet with the sands of seven
    deserts;
Let strong breezes rise,
Washing our ears with the far-off sounds of
    the foam.
Let there be between our faces
Green turf and a branch or two of back-tossed
    trees.
Set firmly over questioning hearts
The deep unquenchable answers of the wind.

II

Let the rain beat in our faces
As we go out on the great quest for life;
Let it blind our eyes with bitter tears,
Tears of the fury of pain.
Let us bear great heavy rains, plodding
Over the furrows of unploughed earth;
For only through long bitterness freely spoken
Can new life come to be, for other men.

III

Let our bodies run laughing in the sunlight,
And sleep under the soft blanket of the stars;
Let us imitate in our movements
The carelessness of trees
That clothe themselves in their fierce glory
Of bud and leaf, that boldly display their
    flowers:
Let us go forth in the day, clad in our might
    like mountains,
To return bearing upon our foreheads the final
    kiss of the night.

IV

Let us bear rich heavy harvests,
Fruits of experience that hang long
In the garden of life in the evening,
Inviting eager lips and eyes.
Yet let us always be children—
Let butterfly moments find us playing;
Let us learn the lesson of the flowers that give
    to the sun
Their petals and their scent.

IF DEATH IS KIND

V

Let the dark king who will crown us
Be welcomed with a kindly smile;
Let him sit beside us in our room,
A friend to whom we give unspoken thoughts.
Death, we will make you but one offering only—
It is enough, you will not need any more:
All of our lives you have waited patiently;
Come then, and take from us this failing
   breath

John Gould Fletcher (1886–1950)

If Death is Kind

Perhaps if Death is kind, and there can be
  returning,
    We will come back to earth some fragrant
      night,
And take these lanes to find the sea, and
  bending
    Breathe the same honeysuckle, low and
      white.

We will come down at night to these
  resounding beaches
    And the long gentle thunder of the sea,
Here for a single hour in the wide starlight
    We shall be happy, for the dead are free.

Sara Teasdale (1884–1933)

from 'I loved her like the leaves'

I loved her like the leaves,
The lush green leaves of spring
That pulled down the willows
on the bank's edge
where we walked
while she was of this world.
I built my life on her.
But man cannot flout
the laws of this world.
To the shimmering wide fields
hidden by the white cloud,
white as white silk scarf
she soared away like the morning bird,
hid from our world like the setting sun.

Kakinomoto Hitomaro (7th century),
translated by Don Paterson

from The Tempest

Our revels now are ended. These our actors,
As I foretold you, were all spirits, and
Are melted into air, into thin air:
And, like the baseless fabric of this vision,
The cloud-capp'd towers, the gorgeous
   palaces,
The solemn temples, the great globe itself,
Yea, all which it inherit, shall dissolve,
And, like this insubstantial pageant faded,
Leave not a rack behind. We are such stuff
As dreams are made on; and our little life
Is rounded with a sleep.

William Shakespeare (1564–1616)

Continuities

Nothing is ever really lost, or can be lost,
No birth, identity, form – no object of the
world.
Nor life, nor force, nor any visible thing;
Appearance must not foil, nor shifted sphere
confuse thy brain.
Ample are time and space – ample the fields of
Nature.
The body, sluggish, aged, cold – the embers
left from earlier fires,
The light in the eye grown dim, shall duly
flame again;
The sun now low in the west rises for
mornings and for noons continual;
To frozen clods ever the spring's invisible law
returns,
With grass and flowers and summer fruits and
corn.

Walt Whitman (1819–1892)

from The Song of Wandering Aengus

Though I am old with wandering
Through hollow lands and hilly lands,
I will find out where she has gone,
And kiss her lips and take her hands;
And walk among long dappled grass,
And pluck till time and times are done
The silver apples of the moon,
The golden apples of the sun.

W. B. Yeats (1865-1939)

from Life

Animula, vagula, blandula

Life! I know not what thou art,
But know that thou and I must part;
And when, or how, or where we met,
I own to me's a secret yet.
But this I know, when thou art fled,
Where'er they lay these limbs, this head,
No clod so valueless shall be,
As all that then remains of me.
O whither, whither dost thou fly,
Where bend unseen thy trackless course,
    And in this strange divorce,
Ah tell where I must seek this compound I?

To the vast ocean of empyreal flame,
    From whence thy essence came,
    Dost thou thy flight pursue, when freed
    From matter's base encumbering weed?
      Or dost thou, hid from sight,
      Wait, like some spell-bound knight,
Through blank oblivious years the' appointed
hour,
To break thy trance and reassume thy power?

Yet canst thou without thought or feeling be?
O say what art thou, when no more thou'rt
  thee?

Life! we've been long together,
Through pleasant and through cloudy
  weather;
    'Tis hard to part when friends are dear;
    Perhaps't will cost a sigh, a tear;
    Then steal away, give little warning,
      Choose thine own time;
Say not Good night, but in some brighter
  clime
      Bid me Good morning.

Anna Laetitia Barbauld (1743–1825)

from War and Peace

"Love hinders death. Love is life. All, everything that I understand, I understand only because I love. Everything is, everything exists, only because I love. Everything is united by it alone. Love is God, and to die means that I, a particle of love, shall return to the general and eternal source."

Leo Tolstoy (1828–1910)

from Song of Myself

A child said *What is the grass?* fetching it to me
    with
        full hands;
How could I answer the child? I do not know
    what it
        is any more than he.

I guess it must be the flag of my disposition,
    out of
        hopeful green stuff woven.

Or I guess it is the handkerchief of the Lord,
A scented gift and remembrancer designedly
    dropt,
Bearing the owner's name someway in the
    corners,
        that we may see and remark, and say
            Whose?

Or I guess the grass is itself a child, the
    produced
        babe of the vegetation.

Or I guess it is a uniform hieroglyphic,
And it means, Sprouting alike in broad zones
  and
    narrow zones,
Growing among black folks as among white,
Kanuck, Tuckahoe, Congressman, Cuff, I give
  them
    the same, I receive them the same.

And now it seems to me the beautiful uncut
  hair of
    graves.

Tenderly will I use you curling grass,
It may be you transpire from the breasts of
  young
    men,
It may be if I had known them I would have
  loved
    them,

It may be you are from old people, or from
  offspring
    taken soon out of their mothers' laps,
And here you are the mothers' laps.

This grass is very dark to be from the white
  heads of
    old mothers,
Darker than the colorless beards of old men,
Dark to come from under the faint red roofs of
    mouths.

O I perceive after all so many uttering
  tongues,
And I perceive they do not come from the
  roofs of
    mouths for nothing.

I wish I could translate the hints about the dead
    young men and women,
And the hints about old men and mothers,
  and the
    offspring taken soon out of their laps.

What do you think has become of the young
  and old
    men?
And what do you think had become of the
  women and
    children?

They are alive and well somewhere,
The smallest sprout shows there is really no
  death,
And if ever there was it led forward life, and
  does not
    wait at the end to arrest it,
And ceas'd the moment life appear'd.

All goes onward and outward, nothing
  collapses,
And to die is different from what any one
  supposed,
    and luckier.

Walt Whitman (1819–1892)

from Little Women

So the spring days came and went, the sky grew clearer, the earth greener, the flowers were up fairly early, and the birds came back in time to say good-by to Beth, who, like a tired but trustful child, clung to the hands that had led her all her life, as Father and Mother guided her tenderly through the Valley of the Shadow, and gave her up to God.

Seldom except in books do the dying utter memorable words, see visions, or depart with beatified countenances, and those who have sped many parting souls know that to most the end comes as naturally and simply as sleep. As Beth had hoped, the "tide went out easily", and in the dark hour before dawn, on the bosom where she had drawn her first breath, she quietly drew her last, with no farewell but one loving look, one little sigh.

Louisa May Alcott (1832–1888)

from In Memoriam, A. H.

You hear the solemn bell
At vespers, when the oriflammes are furled;
And then you know that somewhere in the
  world,
That shines far-off beneath you like a gem,
They think of you, and when you think of
  them
You know that they will wipe away their tears,
And cast aside their fears;
That they will have it so,
And in no otherwise;
That it is well with them because they know,
With faithful eyes,
Fixed forward and turned upwards to the
  skies,
That it is well with you,
Among the chosen few,
Among the very brave, the very true.

Maurice Baring (1874–1945)

from Medley
A Kashmeri Song

The opal lies in the river,
The pearl in the ocean's breast;
Doubt in a grieving bosom,
And faith in a heart at rest.

Fireflies dance in the moon-light,
Peach-leaves dance in the wind;
Dreams and delicate fancies
Dance thro' a poet's mind.

Sweetness dwells in the beehive,
And lives in a maiden's breath;
Joy in the eyes of children
And peace in the hands of Death.

Sarojini Naidu (1879–1949)

'Do not stand at my grave and weep'

Do not stand at my grave and weep;
I am not there. I do not sleep.
I am a thousand winds that blow.
I am the diamond glints on snow.

I am the sunlight on ripened grain.
I am the gentle autumn rain.
When you awaken in the morning's hush
I am the swift uplifting rush

Of quiet birds in circled flight.
I am the soft stars that shine at night.
Do not stand at my grave and cry;
I am not there. I did not die.

Mary Frye (1905–2004)

'Bring us, o Lord God,
at our last awakening'

Bring us, o Lord God, at our last awakening
into the house and gate of Heaven,
to enter into that gate and dwell in that house,
where there shall be no darkness nor dazzling,
   but one equal light;
no noise nor silence, but one equal music;
no fears or hopes, but one equal possession;
no ends or beginnings, but one equal eternity,
in the habitations of thy glory and dominion,
world without end.

John Donne (1572–1631)

from Letter to Thomas Poole,
April 6 1799

Death in a doting old age falls upon my feelings ever as a more hopeless phenomenon than death in infancy; but *nothing* is hopeless. What if the vital force which I sent from my arm into the stone as I flung it in the air and skimmed it upon the water—what if even that did not perish! It was *life!*—it was a particle of *being!*—it was power! and how could it perish? *Life, Power, Being!* Organization may and probably is their *effect*—their *cause* it *cannot* be! I have indulged very curious fancies concerning that force, that swarm of motive powers which I sent out of my body into that stone, and which, one by one, left the untractable or already possessed mass . . .

Samuel Taylor Coleridge (1772–1834)

My Grave

If, when I die, I must be buried, let
No cemetery engulf me—no lone grot,
Where the great palpitating world comes not,
Save when, with heart bowed down and
   eyelids wet,
It pays its last sad melancholy debt
To some out-journeying pilgrim. May my lot
Be rather to lie in some much-used spot,
Where human life, with all its noise and fret,
Throbs on about me. Let the roll of wheels,
With all earth's sounds of pleasure, commerce,
   love,
And rush of hurrying feet surge o'er my head.
Even in my grave I shall be one who feels
Close kinship with the pulsing world above;
And too deep silence would distress me, dead.

Ella Wheeler Wilcox (1850–1919)

Birth and Death

from The Notebooks of Samuel Butler

They are functions one of the other and if you get rid of one you must get rid of the other also. There is birth in death and death in birth. We are always dying and being born again.

Life is the gathering of waves to a head, at death they break into a million fragments each one of which, however, is absorbed at once into the sea of life and helps to form a later generation which comes rolling on till it too breaks.

Samuel Butler (1835–1902)

Lights out

I have come to the borders of sleep,
The unfathomable deep
Forest where all must lose
Their way, however straight,
Or winding, soon or late;
They cannot choose.

Many a road and track
That, since the dawn's first crack,
Up to the forest brink,
Deceived the travellers,
Suddenly now blurs,
And in they sink.

Here love ends,
Despair, ambition ends;
All pleasure and all trouble,
Although most sweet or bitter,
Here ends in sleep that is sweeter
Than tasks most noble.

There is not any book
Or face of dearest look

That I would not turn from now
To go into the unknown
I must enter, and leave, alone,
I know not how.

The tall forest towers;
Its cloudy foliage lowers
Ahead, shelf above shelf;
Its silence I hear and obey
That I may lose my way
And myself.

Edward Thomas (1878–1917)

from One Day's List

But, for you, it shall be forever spring,
And only you shall be forever fearless,
And only you have white, straight, tireless
    limbs,
And only you, where the water-lily swims
Shall walk along the pathways, thro' the
    willows
Of your west.
You who went West,
And only you on silvery twilight pillows
Shall take your rest
In the soft sweet glooms
Of twilight rooms . . .

No. 2 Red Cross Hospital,
Rouen, 7/1/17

Ford Madox Ford (1873–1939)

Heaven-Haven: A nun takes the veil

I have desired to go
Where springs not fail,
To fields where flies no sharp and sided hail
And a few lilies blow.

And I have asked to be
Where no storms come,
Where the green swell is in the havens dumb,
And out of the swing of the sea.

Gerard Manley Hopkins (1844–1889)

There is a Field

Out beyond ideas of wrongdoing
And rightdoing there is a field.
        I'll meet you there.
When the soul lies down in that grass
The world is too full to talk about.

Rumi (1207–1273)

from My Ántonia

There in the sheltered draw-bottom the wind did not blow very hard, but I could hear it singing its humming tune up on the level, and I could see the tall grasses wave. The earth was warm under me, and warm as I crumbled it through my fingers. Queer little red bugs came out and moved in slow squadrons around me. Their backs were polished vermilion, with black spots. I kept as still as I could. Nothing happened. I did not expect anything to happen. I was something that lay under the sun and felt it, like the pumpkins, and I did not want to be anything more. I was entirely happy. Perhaps we feel like that when we die and become a part of something entire, whether it is sun and air, or goodness and knowledge. At any rate, that is happiness; to be dissolved into something complete and great. When it comes to one, it comes as naturally as sleep.

Willa Cather (1873–1947)

from Adonais

Peace, peace! he is not dead, he doth not sleep –
He hath awakened from the dream of life –
'Tis we, who lost in stormy visions, keep
With phantoms an unprofitable strife,
And in mad trance, strike with our spirit's
  knife
Invulnerable nothings. – *We* decay
Like corpses in a charnel; fear and grief
Convulse us and consume us day by day,
And cold hopes swarm like worms within our
  living clay.

He has outsoared the shadow of our night;
Envy and calumny and hate and pain,
And that unrest which men miscall delight,
Can touch him not and torture not again;
From the contagion of the world's slow stain
He is secure, and now can never mourn
A heart grown cold, a head grown gray in vain;
Nor, when the spirit's self has ceased to burn,
With sparkless ashes load an unlamented urn.

Percy Bysshe Shelley (1792–1822)

from Cymbeline

Fear no more the heat o'the sun,
　　Nor the furious winter's rages;
Thou thy worldly task hast done,
　　Home art gone, and ta'en thy wages:
Golden lads and girls all must,
　　As chimney-sweepers, come to dust.

Fear no more the frown o'the great,
　　Thou art past the tyrant's stroke:
Care no more to clothe and eat;
　　To thee the reed is as the oak;
The sceptre, learning, physic, must
　　All follow this, and come to dust.

Fear no more the lightning-flash,
　　Nor the all-dreaded thunder-stone;
Fear not slander, censure rash;
　　Thou hast finish'd joy and moan:
All lovers young, all lovers must
　　Consign to thee, and come to dust.

No exorciser harm thee!
　　Nor no witchcraft charm thee!

Ghost unlaid forbear thee!
　　Nothing ill come near thee!
Quiet consummation have;
　　And renowned be thy grave!

William Shakespeare (1564–1616)

FREEDOM

Freedom

Give me the long, straight road before me,
    A clear, cold day with a nipping air,
Tall, bare trees to run on beside me,
    A heart that is light and free from care.
Then let me go! – I care not whither
    My feet may lead, for my spirit shall be
Free as the brook that flows to the river,
    Free as the river that flows to the sea.

Olive Runner

from Last Verses

The seas are quiet when the winds give o'er;
So calm are we when passions are no more.
For then we know how vain it was to boast
Of fleeting things, so certain to be lost.
Clouds of affection from our younger eyes
Conceal that emptiness which age descries.

The soul's dark cottage, battered and decayed,
Lets in new light through chinks that Time
  has made
Stronger, by weakness, wiser men become
As they draw near to their eternal home.
Leaving the old, both worlds at once they view
That stand upon the threshold of the new.

Edmund Waller (1606–1687)

from In the Mountains

Now I am going very happy to bed, for I have passed the test. The whole of the walk to the larches, and the whole of the way back, and all the time I was sitting there, what I felt was simply gratitude—gratitude for the beautiful past times I have had. I found I couldn't help it. It was as natural as breathing. I wasn't lonely. Everybody I have loved and shall never see again was with me. And all day, the whole of the wonderful day of beauty, I was able in that bright companionship to forget the immediate grief, the aching wretchedness, that brought me up here to my mountains as a last hope.

Elizabeth von Arnim (1866–1941)

Turn again

If I should die and leave you here awhile,
Be not like others, sore undone, who keep
Long vigils by the silent dust, and weep.
For my sake, turn again to life and smile,
Nerving thy heart and trembling hand to do
Something to comfort weaker hearts than
   thine.
Complete those dear unfinished tasks of mine,
And I perchance may therein comfort you!

Mary Lee Hall (1843–1927)

In Blackwater Woods

Look, the trees
are turning
their own bodies
into pillars

of light,
are giving off the rich
fragrance of cinnamon
and fulfillment,

the long tapers
of cattails
are bursting and floating away over
the blue shoulders

of the ponds,
and every pond,
no matter what its
name is, is

nameless now.
Every year

everything
I have ever learned

in my lifetime
leads back to this: the fires
and the black river of loss
whose other side

is salvation,
whose meaning
none of us will ever know.
To live in this world

you must be able
to do three things:
to love what is mortal;
to hold it

against your bones knowing
your own life depends on it;
and, when the time comes to let it go,
to let it go.

Mary Oliver (1935–2019)

A Celtic blessing

Deep peace of the running wave to you,
Deep peace of the flowing air to you,
Deep peace of the quiet earth to you,
Deep peace of the shining stars to you,
Deep peace of the Son of Peace to you.
May the road rise to meet you;
May the wind be always at your back;
May the sun shine warm upon your face;
May the rains fall softly upon your fields.
　　　Until we meet again,
May God hold you in the hollow of His hand.

Anon.

Everything you see

Everything you see has its roots in the unseen
   world.
      The forms may change, yet the essence
         remains the same.
Every wonderful sight will vanish, every sweet
   word will fade,
      But do not be disheartened,
The source they come from is eternal, growing,
      Branching out, giving new life and new joy.
Why do you weep?
      The source is within you
And this whole world is springing up from it.

Rumi (1207–1273)

Peace, my heart

Peace, my heart, let the time for the parting
  be sweet.
Let it not be a death but completeness.
Let love melt into memory and pain into
  songs.
Let the flight through the sky end in the
  folding of
    the wings over the nest.
Let the last touch of your hands be gentle
  like the
    flower of the night.
Stand still, O Beautiful End, for a moment,
  and say
    your last words in silence.
I bow to you and hold up my lamp to light
  you on
    your way.

Rabindranath Tagore (1861–1941)

Elegy Before Death

There will be rose and rhododendron
    When you are dead and under ground;
Still will be heard from white syringas
    Heavy with bees, a sunny sound;

Still will the tamaracks be raining
    After the rain has ceased, and still
Will there be robins in the stubble,
    Brown sheep upon the warm green hill.

Spring will not ail nor autumn falter;
    Nothing will know that you are gone,
Saving alone some sullen plough-land
    None but yourself sets foot upon;

Saving the may-weed and the pig-weed
    Nothing will know that you are dead,—
These, and perhaps a useless wagon
    Standing beside some tumbled shed.

Oh, there will pass with your great passing
    Little of beauty not your own,—

Only the light from common water,
Only the grace from simple stone!

Edna St. Vincent Millay (1892–1950)

'Death stands above me'

Death stands above me, whispering low
  I know not what into my ear:
Of his strange language all I know
  Is, there is not a word of fear.

Walter Savage Landor (1775–1864)

Farewell, sweet dust

Now I have lost you, I must scatter
All of you on the air henceforth;
Not that to me it can ever matter
But it's only fair to the rest of the earth.

Now especially, when it is winter
And the sun's not half as bright as it was,
Who wouldn't be glad to find a splinter
That once was you, in the frozen grass?

Snowflakes, too, will be softer feathered,
Clouds, perhaps, will be whiter plumed;
Rain, whose brilliance you caught and
    gathered,
Purer silver have resumed.

Farewell, sweet dust; I never was a miser:
Once, for a minute, I made you mine:
Now you are gone, I am none the wiser
But the leaves of the willow are as bright as
    wine.

Elinor Wylie (1885–1928)

No Funeral Gloom

No funeral gloom, my dears, when I am gone,
Corpse-gazing, tears, black raiment, graveyard
  grimness.
Think of me as withdrawn into the dimness,
Yours still, you mine.
Remember all the best of our past moments
    and forget
      the rest,
And so to where I wait come gently on.

Ellen Terry (1847–1928)

'Never weather-beaten Sail'

Never weather-beaten Sail more willing bent
   to shore,
Never tired Pilgrim's limbs affected slumber
   more,
Than my wearied spright now longs to fly out
   of my troubled breast.
     O come quickly, sweetest Lord, and take
      my soul to rest.

Ever-blooming are the joys of Heav'n's high
   paradise,
Cold age deafs not there our ears, nor vapour
   dims our eyes:
Glory there the Sun outshines, whose beams
   the blessed only see;
     O come quickly, glorious Lord, and raise
      my spright to thee.

Thomas Campion (1567–1620)

Freedom

I will not follow you, my bird,
    I will not follow you.
I would not breathe a word, my bird,
    To bring thee here anew.

I love the free in thee, my bird,
    The lure of freedom drew;
The light you fly toward, my bird,
    I fly with thee unto.

And there we yet will meet, my bird,
    Though far I go from you
Where in the light outpoured, my bird,
    Are love and freedom too.

George William Russell (1867–1935)

'If I should go before the rest of you'

If I should go before the rest of you
Break not a flower nor inscribe a stone,
Nor when I'm gone speak in a Sunday voice
But be the usual selves that I have known.
　　Weep if you must,
　　Parting is hell,
　　But life goes on,
　　So sing as well.

Joyce Grenfell (1910–1979)

from The Wind in the Willows

He saw clearly how plain and simple – how
narrow, even – it all was, but clearly, too, how
much it all meant to him, and the special value
of some such anchorage in one's existence. He
did not at all want to abandon the new life and
its splendid spaces, to turn his back on sun and
air and all they offered him and creep home and
stay there; the upper world was all too strong, it
called to him still, even down there, and he
knew he must return to the larger stage. But it
was good to think he had this to come back to,
this place which was all his own, these things
which were so glad to see him again and could
always be counted upon for the same simple
welcome.

Kenneth Grahame (1859–1932)

from The Old Curiosity Shop

Oh! it is hard to take to heart the lesson that such deaths will teach, but let no man reject it, for it is one that all must learn, and is a mighty, universal Truth. When Death strikes down the innocent and young, for every fragile form from which he lets the panting spirit free, a hundred virtues rise, in shapes of mercy, charity, and love, to walk the world, and bless it. Of every tear that sorrowing mortals shed on such green graves, some good is born, some gentler nature comes. In the Destroyer's steps there spring up bright creations that defy his power, and his dark path becomes a way of light to Heaven.

Charles Dickens (1812–1870)

from Chamber Music
XXXIV

Sleep now, O sleep now,
 O you unquiet heart!
A voice crying "Sleep now"
 Is heard in my heart.

The voice of the winter
 Is heard at the door.
O sleep, for the winter
 Is crying "Sleep no more."

My kiss will give peace now
 And quiet to your heart—
Sleep on in peace now,
 O you unquiet heart!

James Joyce (1882–1941)

from The Death of the Moth

After perhaps a seventh attempt he slipped from the wooden ledge and fell, fluttering his wings, on to his back on the window sill. The helplessness of his attitude roused me. It flashed upon me that he was in difficulties; he could no longer raise himself; his legs struggled vainly. But, as I stretched out a pencil, meaning to help him to right himself, it came over me that the failure and awkwardness were the approach of death. I laid the pencil down again.

The legs agitated themselves once more. I looked as if for the enemy against which he struggled. I looked out of doors. What had happened there? Presumably it was midday, and work in the fields had stopped. Stillness and quiet had replaced the previous animation. The birds had taken themselves off to feed in the brooks. The horses stood still. Yet the power was there all the same, massed outside indifferent, impersonal, not attending to anything in particular. Somehow it was opposed to the little hay-coloured moth. It was useless to try to do anything. One could only watch the extraordinary efforts made by those tiny legs against an oncoming doom which could, had it chosen, have submerged an entire city, not merely a city, but masses of human beings; nothing, I knew had any chance against death. Nevertheless after a pause of exhaustion the legs fluttered again. It was superb this last protest, and so frantic that he succeeded at last in righting himself. One's sympathies, of course, were all on the side of life. Also, when there was nobody to care or to know, this gigantic effort on the part of an insignificant little moth, against a power of such magnitude, to retain what no one else valued or desired to keep, moved one strangely. Again, somehow, one saw life, a pure bead. I lifted the pencil again, useless though I knew it to be. But even as I did so, the unmistakable tokens of death showed themselves. The body relaxed, and instantly grew stiff. The struggle was over. The insignificant little creature now knew death. As I looked at the dead moth, this minute wayside triumph of so great a force over so mean an antagonist filled me with wonder. Just as life had been strange a few minutes before, so death was now

as strange. The moth having righted himself
now lay most decently and uncomplainingly
composed. O yes, he seemed to say, death is
stronger than I am.

Virginia Woolf (1882–1941)

from Peter Pan

Peter was not quite like other boys; but he was afraid at last. A tremor ran through him, like a shudder passing over the sea; but on the sea one shudder follows another till there are hundreds of them, and Peter felt just the one. Next moment he was standing erect on the rock again, with that smile on his face and a drum beating within him. It was saying, 'To die will be an awfully big adventure.'

J. M. Barrie (1860–1937)

Crossing the Bar

Sunset and evening star,
    And one clear call for me!
And may there be no moaning of the bar,
    When I put out to sea,

But such a tide as moving seems asleep,
    Too full for sound and foam,
When that which drew from out the boundless
  deep
    Turns again home.

Twilight and evening bell,
    And after that the dark!
And may there be no sadness of farewell,
    When I embark;

For tho' from out our bourne of Time and
  Place
    The flood may bear me far,
I hope to see my Pilot face to face
    When I have crost the bar.

Alfred, Lord Tennyson (1809–1892)

Song

When I am dead, my dearest,
Sing no sad songs for me;
Plant thou no roses at my head,
Nor shady cypress tree:
Be the green grass above me
With showers and dewdrops wet;
And if thou wilt, remember,
And if thou wilt, forget.

I shall not see the shadow,
I shall not feel the rain;
I shall not hear the nightingale
Sing on, as if in pain;
And dreaming through the twilight
That doth not rise nor set,
Haply I may remember,
And haply may forget.

Christina Rossetti (1830–1894)

from In Memoriam A. H. H.
CXXXI

O living will that shalt endure
When all that seems shall suffer shock,
Rise in the spiritual rock,
Flow thro' our deeds and make them pure,

That we may lift from out of dust
A voice as unto him that hears,
A cry above the conquer's years
To one that with us works, and trust,

With faith that comes of self-control,
The truths that never can be proved
Until we close with all we loved,
And all we flow from, soul in soul.

Alfred, Lord Tennyson (1809–1892)

'Why hold on to just one life'

Why hold on to just one life
till it is filthy and threadbare?
The sun dies eternally
and wastes a thousand lives each instant.
God has decreed a life for you
and He will give another,
then another and another.

Rumi (1207–1273)

To Every Thing There Is a Season

To every thing there is a season,
and a time to every purpose under the heaven:
A time to be born, and a time to die;
A time to plant, and a time to pluck up that
  which is
    planted;
A time to kill, and a time to heal;
A time to break down, and a time to build up;
A time to weep, and a time to laugh;
A time to mourn, and a time to dance;
A time to cast away stones, and a time to
  gather
    stones together;
A time to embrace, and a time to refrain from
    embracing;
A time to get, and a time to lose;
A time to keep, and a time to cast away;
A time to rend, and a time to sew;
A time to keep silence, and a time to speak;
A time to love, and a time to hate;
A time of war, and a time of peace.

Book of Ecclesiastes

How Do I Love Thee?

How do I love thee? Let me count the ways,
I love thee to the depth and breadth and
  height
My soul can reach, when feeling out of sight
For the ends of Being and ideal Grace.

I love thee to the level of everyday's
Most quiet need, by sun and candlelight.
I love thee freely, as men strive for Right;
I love thee purely, as they turn from Praise.

I love thee with the passion put to use
In my old griefs, and with my childhood's
  faith.
I love thee with a love I seemed to lose

With my lost saints – I love thee with the
  breath,
Smiles, tears, of all my life! – and, if God
  choose
I shall but love thee better after death.

Elizabeth Barrett Browning (1806–1861)

from The Garden of Proserpine

From too much love of living,
    From hope and fear set free,
We thank with brief thanksgiving
    Whatever gods may be
That no life lives for ever;
That dead men rise up never;
That even the weariest river
    Winds somewhere safe to sea.

Algernon Charles
Swinburne (1837–1909)

'I have seen death too often'

I have seen death too often to believe in death.
It is not an ending, but a withdrawal.
As one who finishes a long journey
Stills the motor, turns off the lights,
Steps from his car,
And walks up the path to the home that
   awaits him.

Anon.

Index of Poets and Authors

Alcott, Louisa May   123
Anon.   102, 149, 174
Auden, W. H.   3
Austen, Cassandra   12

Barbauld, Anna Laetitia   116
Baring, Maurice   124
Barrie, J. M.   166
Barton, Bernard   70
Book of Ecclesiastes   171
Brontë, Anne   35
Brontë, Emily   43
Browning, Elizabeth Barrett   63, 172
Browning, Robert   103
Burns, Robert   85
Butler, Samuel   130
Byron, Lord   6

Campion, Thomas   157
Cather, Willa   136
Chief Tecumseh of the Shawnee Nation   86
Clare, John   39
Coleridge, Mary   72
Coleridge, Samuel Taylor   128
Cowper, William   5

de Saint-Exupéry, Antoine   52
Dickens, Charles   161
Dickinson, Emily   68

Donne, John 127
Dryden, John 92
Dyer, Catherine 16

Fletcher, John Gould 105
Foley, James W. 64
Ford, Ford Madox 133
Frost, Robert 76
Frye, Mary 126

Gibran, Kahlil 22, 81
Grahame, Kenneth 160
Grenfell, Joyce 159

Hall, Mary Lee 146
Hardy, Thomas 7
Harrold, A. F. 31
Heguri, Lady 21
Herrick, Robert 19
Hitomaro, Kakinomoto 112
Holland, Henry Scott 84
Hopkins, Gerard Manley 134
Housman, A. E. 98

James, Henry 9
Johnson, Samuel 69
Joyce, James 162

Kingsley, Charles 100

Landor, Walter Savage 154
Lawrence, D. H. 56

Mackay, Charles   75
Mansfield, Katherine   59
Mew, Charlotte   41
Meynell, Alice   13
Millay, Edna St. Vincent   10, 152
Montgomery, Lucy Maud   24
Mu, Tu   8

Naidu, Sarojini   77, 125

Oliver, Mary   147
Owen, Wilfred   54

Penn, William   48
Pliny the Younger   27
Po, Li   71
Proust, Marcel   49

Raleigh, Sir Walter   47
Rossetti, Christina   62, 168
Rumi   135, 150, 170
Runner, Olive   143
Russell, George William   158

Shakespeare, William   23, 40, 45, 67, 113, 138
Shelley, Percy Bysshe   30, 57, 137
Smith, Lanta Wilson   33
Stevenson, Robert Louis   50, 101
Swinburne, Algernon Charles   173

Tagore, Rabindranath   60, 151
Teasdale, Sara   111

Tennyson, Alfred, Lord   29, 167, 169
Terry, Ellen   156
Thackeray, William Makepeace   95
Thomas, Dylan   79
Thomas, Edward   131
Thoreau, Henry David   90
Tolstoy, Leo   118
Twain, Mark   42

Van Dyke, Henry   83
von Arnim, Elizabeth   145

Walcott, Derek   17
Waller, Edmund   144
Whitman, Walt   114, 119
Wilcox, Ella Wheeler   93, 129
Wilde, Oscar   15
Wollstonecraft, Mary   46
Woolf, Virginia   58, 88, 163
Wordsworth, William   51, 55, 89
Wylie, Elinor   155

Yeats, W. B.   91, 115
Yu, Li   26

Index of First Lines

A child said What is the grass? fetching it to me
   with 119

A slumber did my spirit seal; 55

A thousand years, you said, 21

After great pain a formal feeling comes – 68

After perhaps a seventh attempt he slipped from the
   wooden ledge and fell, fluttering his wings, on to
   his back on the window sill. 163

All are not taken; there are left behind 63

An honest man here lies at rest, 85

Beloved, thou art like a tune that idle fingers 13

Bright is the ring of words 50

Bring us, o Lord God, at our last awakening 127

But, for you, it shall be forever spring, 133

... But true love is a durable fire, 47

Death in a doting old age falls upon my feelings ever
   as a more hopeless phenomenon than death in
   infancy; 128

Death is nothing at all. 84

Deep peace of the running wave to you, 149

Did it matter then, she asked herself, walking towards
   Bond Street, did it matter that she must inevitably
   cease completely; 88

Do not go gentle into that good night, 79

Do not stand at my grave and weep; 126

Drop a pebble in the water: just a splash, and it is
   gone; 64

Everything you see has its roots in the unseen
    world.   150

Fear death?—to feel the fog in my throat,   103
Fear no more the heat o'the sun,   138
From too much love of living,   173

Give me the long, straight road before me,   143
Grief fills the room up of my absent child: 23

Half my friends are dead.   17
Happy the man, and happy he alone,   92
Hard is that heart, and unsubdued by love,   5
He saw clearly how plain and simple – how narrow,
    even – it all was, but clearly, too, how much it all
    meant to him, and the special value of some such
    anchorage in one's existence.   160
How do I love thee? Let me count the ways,   172

I am every moment reflecting what a valuable friend,
    what an excellent man, I am deprived of   27
I am not afraid that I shall exaggerate the value and
    significance of life, but that I shall not be up to the
    occasion which it is.   90
I am not resigned to the shutting away of loving
    hearts in the hard ground.   10
I have come to the borders of sleep,   131
I have desired to go   134
I have lived and I have loved;   75
I have lost a treasure, such a sister, such a friend as
    never can have been surpassed   12

I have seen death too often to believe in death. 174

I loved her like the leaves, 112

I miss you 31

I thought no more was needed 91

I will not follow you, my bird, 158

If I should die and leave you here awhile, 146

If I should go before the rest of you 159

If, when I die, I must be buried, let 129

It is only the recumbent who know what, after all,
    nature is at no pains to conceal—that she in the
    end will conquer; 58

It was beautiful 60

Last night for the first time since you were dead 59

Laugh, and the world laughs with you; 93

Let the wind come, 105

Life of my life, take not so soone thy flight, 19

Life! I know not what thou art, 116

Live your life that the fear of death 86

Look, the trees 147

"Love hinders death. 118

Love lives beyond the tomb 39

Men say the world is full of fear and hate, 77

Move him into the sun – 54

Music, when soft voices die, 57

My dearest dust, could not thy hasty day 16

Nature's first green is gold, 76

Never weather-beaten Sail more willing bent to
    shore, 157

No coward soul is mine   43
No funeral gloom, my dears, when I am gone,   156
No longer mourn for me when I am dead   45
Not, how did he die, but how did he live?   102
Nothing is ever really lost, or can be lost,   114
Now I am going very happy to bed, for I have passed
   the test.   145
Now I have lost you, I must scatter   155

O living will that shalt endure   169
'O, they have robbed me of the hope   35
Oh! it is hard to take to heart the lesson that such
   deaths will teach, but let no man reject it, for it is
   one that all must learn, and is a mighty, universal
   Truth.   161
Once in the wind of morning   96
Our revels now are ended. These our actors,   113
Out beyond ideas of wrongdoing   135

Peace, my heart, let the time for the parting be
   sweet.   151
Peace, peace! he is not dead, he doth not
   sleep –   137
'People have stars but they're not all the same.   52
Perhaps if Death is kind, and there can be
   returning,   111
Peter was not quite like other boys; but he was afraid
   at last.   166
Prosperity, pleasure, and success, may be rough of
   grain and common in fibre, but sorrow is the most
   sensitive of all created things.   15

Remember me when I am gone away,   62

Seventeen years ago you said   41
Silently I climb the Western Tower,   26
Sleep now, O sleep now,   162
So deep in love, we seem without passion.   8
So the spring days came and went,   123
So, we'll go no more a-roving   6
Some hang above the tombs,   72
Stop all the clocks, cut off the telephone,   3
Sunset and evening star,   167

The clear spring reflects the thin, wide-spreading
    pine-tree—   71
The dead are like the stars by day,   70
The opal lies in the river,   125
The pine and fir woods, left entirely to Nature,
    display an endless variety;   46
The seas are quiet when the winds give o'er;   144
The world is a looking-glass, and gives back to every
    man the reflection of his own face.   95
There in the sheltered draw-bottom the wind did not
    blow very hard, but I could hear it singing its
    humming tune up on the level, and I could see the
    tall grasses wave.   136
There will be rose and rhododendron   152
They are functions one of the other and if you get rid
    of one you must get rid of the other also.   130
They that love beyond the world, cannot be
    separated by it.   48
This is our day of mourning.   42

This is the spot: – how mildly does the sun   89
Those that have loved longest love best.   69
Thou wert the morning star among the living,   30
Though I am old with wandering   115
Time is too slow for those who wait,   83
To every thing there is a season,   171
To-morrow, and to-morrow, and to-morrow,   40
Two days afterwards they carried Matthew Cuthbert
    over his homestead threshold and away from the
    fields he had tilled and the orchards he had loved
    and the trees he had planted;   24

Under the wide and starry sky,   101

We all live together, and those of us who love and
    know, live so most.   9
We say at times that something may survive of a man
    after his death, if the man was an artist and took a
    certain amount of pains with his work.   49
What though the radiance which was once so
    bright   51
When all the world is young, lad,   100
When I am dead, my dearest,   168
When some great sorrow like a mighty river,   33
When to the sessions of sweet silent thought   67
Why does the thin grey strand   56
Why hold on to just one life   170
Wild bird, whose warble, liquid sweet,   29

You did not walk with me   7
You hear the solemn bell   124

You would know the secret of death.   81
Your pain is the breaking of the shell that encloses
   your understanding.   22

Permissions acknowledgements